J

Soyer   79 12934

The adventures of Yemimi,
and other stories

 DISCARD

CHILDREN'S DEPARTMENT

CENTRAL ARKANSAS LIBRARY SYSTEM
LITTLE ROCK PUBLIC LIBRARY
700 LOUISIANA
LITTLE ROCK, ARKANSAS

D1028969

THE ADVENTURES
OF YEMIMA

THE ADVENTURES OF YEMIMA

AND OTHER STORIES ❧ by Abraham Soyer

TRANSLATED BY REBECCA S. BEAGLE AND REBECCA SOYER

INTRODUCTION BY PETER S. BEAGLE

Illustrated by Raphael Soyer

THE VIKING PRESS, NEW YORK

CENTRAL ARKANSAS LIBRARY SYSTEM
LITTLE ROCK PUBLIC LIBRARY
700 LOUISIANA
LITTLE ROCK, ARKANSAS

First Edition
Illustrations Copyright © Raphael Soyer, 1979
Translation Copyright © Rebecca Soyer and Rebecca S. Beagle, 1979
All rights reserved
First published in 1979 by The Viking Press
625 Madison Avenue, New York, N.Y. 10022
Published simultaneously in Canada by
Penguin Books Canada Limited
Printed in U.S.A.
1 2 3 4 5 83 82 81 80 79

Originally published in Hebrew by Shilo Publishing Company,
Tel Aviv, Professor Zevi Scharfstein, editor and publisher.

Library of Congress Cataloging in Publication Data
Soyer, Abraham. The adventures of Yemima, and other stories.
Summary: A courageous little girl who outwits a wolf,
an unhappy king who wants a son, and a good woman who
is rewarded with flying money are included in this
collection of Hebrew fables.
1. Fables, Hebrew. [1. Fables] I. Soyer, Raphael. II. Title.
PZ8.2.S64Ad   [Fic]   78-26017   ISBN 0-670-10616-X

For the grandchildren of Abraham Soyer—
David, Ora, Mary, Avi, Peter, Ezra, Naomi, and Daniel,
and their children

ACKNOWLEDGMENT

We would like to acknowledge with deep appreciation the help given us by our friend Paula Jacobs, who typed and retyped each story, who made many valuable suggestions, and who was a constant source of encouragement.

These stories were originally published in Hebrew by Shilo Publishing Company, Professor Zevi Scharfstein, editor and publisher. The Publishers gratefully acknowledge the cooperation of Mrs. Rose Scharfstein in making this material available for the English translation.

Foreword

᪥ I NEVER MET MY GRANDFATHER ABRAHAM SOYER—HE DIED WHEN I
was ten months old—but that doesn't mean I didn't know him. He was
a continuing presence in our Bronx apartment during my childhood:
his thin, white-bearded face, wise and wondering at the same time,
looked at me out of portraits and sketches by his artist sons, and I would
stare back at him for hours, thinking myself into the paintings (as I
could do so easily then, and so rarely can today), inventing my grandfather, the only person, I had been told, who could quiet me when I
was a crying baby. That was all I knew *about* him in those days, but I
always knew him.

When I grew older, there were the stories. My mother would read
them aloud to me and to my younger brother Daniel, translating as she
went along. The Grimm and Perrault stories that I learned at school
were always fairy tales, as much as I loved them. These were different.

Perhaps the difference lies in the hunger that is never far from the
surface of these stories, when it isn't actually the main character. The
people in my grandfather's tales are never safe from hunger, never
truly secure beyond the next meal or two; they dwell in a landscape

CENTRAL ARKANSAS LIBRARY SYSTEM
LITTLE ROCK PUBLIC LIBRARY
700 LOUISIANA
LITTLE ROCK, ARKANSAS

of starvation, and no roads lead out of it. Even the wild animals who menace them are having a hard time—my grandfather's lions and wolves and foxes might as well be human beings driven to banditry and murder by the desperation of their families and the silence of God. I always felt sorry for those animals, even the wickedest of them, and I still do.

But the remarkable and wonderful thing, to me, is that the stories are filled with such hopefulness, such a belief in the miracle of justice. The ragged beggar sleeping in front of the stove so often turns out to be an angel; the woman who unselfishly shares the little she has finds herself rewarded with exactly as much as she needs; kindness eventually does come to the attention of the universe, and greed and cruelty must overreach and destroy themselves by their own natures. It cannot have been an easy trust for a poor Russian Jew to sustain at any time, and perhaps it's impossible for anyone anywhere now. But it was always the best thing to believe, true or not—in a way, it was better than the truth, as human beings sometimes are.

Hello, Grandfather, *zayde* Abraham. Here you are in another language, another world, more than a hundred years after your birth, offering Yemima to today's children. Will they like her? I wonder. Will she and her world mean anything at all to them? I think so. A story is still a story, even now; magic is still magic, children are still children— and hope is still, somehow, hope.

Peter S. Beagle

Contents

◈◈◈◈◈◈◈◈◈◈◈◈◈◈◈◈◈◈◈◈◈◈◈◈◈◈◈◈◈◈◈

The Adventures of Yemima

◥ THERE WAS ONCE A LITTLE GIRL NAMED YEMIMA, WHO LIVED WITH HER mother and father and grandmother and Dvora, the maid, in a house on a hill outside of town. Behind the house there was a garden with a little gate that led to the river. Yemima loved that river and the fish that swam in it. Every morning she would get up very early, take some slices of bread from the kitchen, crumble them in her hands, and throw them out on the water. All kinds of fish—big and little, flat and round, fat and thin—would come swimming from all parts of the river and eat the bread that Yemima threw them. And thus Yemima and the fish became great friends.

One day when the family had finished the evening meal and Yemima was getting ready for bed, her father said to her, "Mima, dear, I have something important to tell you. Don't go to the river tomorrow morning to feed the fish as you usually do."

"But why, Father?" Yemima asked.

"Because there is a big wolf down there among the bushes and reeds at the edge of the river. He is watching for you—and he is a very hungry wolf."

CENTRAL ARKANSAS LIBRARY SYSTEM
LITTLE ROCK PUBLIC LIBRARY
700 LOUISIANA
LITTLE ROCK, ARKANSAS

J 79-12934

"There is a big wolf down there among the bushes and reeds . . ."

"A wolf! Where did he come from?"

"He came from the thick forest on the other side of the river."

"Really? Does the wolf know how to swim?"

"No, my little Mima. The wolf does not swim—he came on foot. Far from here there is a big bridge near the mill. The mill was built for the people of the village who come to grind their wheat. That is the bridge the wolf crossed to come here."

Yemima was quiet and didn't answer. Father kissed her, said her night prayer with her, and she went to bed.

Very early the next morning, while the household was still asleep, Yemima rose, quietly slipped out of bed, tiptoed in her bare feet so as not to awaken anybody, closed the door carefully behind her, and went into the kitchen. She took some slices of bread, walked out into the garden, opened the garden gate, and hurried along the dew-covered path to the river. There she threw her crumbs of bread out upon the water to feed the fish, as was her custom each day.

It was a very beautiful morning. The sun had just begun to shine. On the river were small, gentle ripples. A quiet breeze was blowing and ruffled Yemima's curls.

Sinking her feet into the damp sand, Yemima sat down on a stone and waited for the fish to come and get their breakfast.

Suddenly she heard from behind her a thick, harsh voice.

"Mima! I am going to eat you!"

Yemima turned quickly, and there stood the wolf right at her side. His big mouth was open, his large teeth gleamed, his wicked eyes were glaring hungrily at her, and he looked very terrible.

But Yemima was a very clever little girl. She didn't become confused or frightened. Not even one little tiny step did she take backward, but turning to the wolf, completely calm and smiling, she said, "You want to eat me? Very well. But how will you eat me? I'm so dirty—I haven't even washed my face and hands this morning. And look, just *look* at my feet. How dirty and sandy they are! Let me run into the river and wash my hands and feet, and then I will come to you washed and clean and you can eat me."

"You are quite right," answered the wolf. "Cleanliness is indeed a very good quality. Doctors always urge us to keep clean, and I myself— I like cleanliness very much. Hurry, then, and wash yourself and come right back to me, because I am very hungry."

"Just one minute, my dear Wolf, one little tiny minute," cried Yemima as she ran toward the river.

Pretending to be washing herself, she softly called to her friend Dagon, the dolphin, who was swimming not far from her.

"Dear, dear Dagon," she whispered, "see that wolf there on the bank? He's waiting to eat me. Please help me, Dagon. Save me!"

"Hurry, get on my back, and I will take you across the river." Dagon loved Yemima very much, as she loved him and all his friends and relations.

She got on Dagon's back, and in hardly any time at all she was on the other side of the river where the great forest stood.

The wolf saw what had happened, and he ground his teeth in anger. He raised his head and roared and said, "Wait, you little deceiver! You are not safe yet. I will cross the bridge and get you. The forest, Yemima, belongs to me!"

No sooner had Yemima gotten off the dolphin's back at the river's edge than she heard another voice—this one sweet and charming. She

4

She got on Dagon's back . . .

turned and saw a fox coming toward her, mincing and dancing and swishing his tail.

"Good morning, Yemima," he said most politely. "Is everything all right? What are you doing here so early in the morning?"

"I will explain everything, my dear good Fox," cried Yemima, "but first won't you save me from this wolf who is pursuing me? Do you see him? There he is, galloping across the bridge. He wants to catch me and eat me."

"He will not catch you," answered the fox in a loud voice, but to himself he said, "Not he, but I. What a feast she will be for my wife and my poor little hungry children!"

So, swishing his tail and speaking sweetly, he said, "For you, Yemima, dear child, I am ready and willing to go through fire and water. I have a big den in this forest. Come, let me take you there. You can play with my little ones while my wife goes to your house to assure your parents that you are safe with me, for they surely must be worried about you.

"And I? I will go to meet the wolf. I will talk to him and flatter him and entice him into the hunters' trap room. I will get him in there, and there he will remain forever. Now hurry and get on my back so I can take you to my house."

Yemima could see that the fox was lying, and she was frightened. "But—I wish—it would be better if you took me straight to my mama and papa. . . . I want my grandma." She began to cry.

"Oh, Yemima, you are talking like a little baby! You are such a bright child, you must understand that, first of all, we must get rid of the wolf, and in order to do that we must hurry and get him into that trap room. If not, he will overtake us, and both of us, you and I, will be his victims. Afterward, toward evening, I will come and take you to your parents' house."

"And I—I will g-g-give you a beautiful p-p-present," said Yemima through her tears. "A big hen—if only—"

"Oh, Mima," answered the fox, "do you think I'm doing this for a reward or for payment? You foolish little girl. I'm doing this because I'm your friend and your parents' friend and I love you and I want to save you from this bad wolf."

So Yemima got up on the back of the fox, and as he hurried along he told her about the trap room into which he was planning to entice the wolf.

"In the middle of the forest," the fox explained, "the hunters have built for us animals a trap room. It is like a little house. In this house

6

there are two rooms, one within the other, and an iron wall between them. In the inside room they have placed a live goat. The outside room is empty and has a door which is always shut. It is made in such a way that whoever goes in cannot come out, for immediately the door closes behind him forever. To this room I will bring the wolf and will persuade him to enter, for I will tell him that you, Yemima, are in there hiding from him. He will surely believe me because he will hear the footsteps of the goat and will think that it is you walking inside back and forth. And when he enters—immediately the door will shut behind him—and the wolf will remain in the room imprisoned forever. Then I will hurry to you and take you to your father's home, and we'll tell him where the wolf is. I know your father has a rifle. He will come and kill the wolf, and he will have the fur of the animal for a nice warm coat this winter."

When Yemima said nothing, the fox went along, talking to her and dancing as he walked in order to jog her a little to raise her spirits, dancing and talking to calm her fears until he came to his den. Yemima got off the fox's back, and he took her into his cave, introduced her to his little children, and told them to play with Yemima and amuse her. But quietly he whispered to them, "Watch out for this little girl because she is sly and very clever. Guard her well, and tonight when Mother and I return we will have a good feast—" The little foxes rejoiced and swished their tails, and the fox ran off to meet the wolf.

And there was the wolf coming toward him, looking very angry. "Good day, Brother Wolf," called the fox. "Why do you look so angry this morning? Stop worrying— look, the sun—"

"Sun, shmun. What good is the sun to me and of what use is it when there's nothing to eat? My little wolves are hungry. My wife is constantly sullen and angry and complaining. My den is empty—a dry bone you will not find in it." He shook his head. "And to think, only this morning

I had that little Yemima. She was practically in my paws—but she got away, the sly one. Old fool that I am, I was persuaded. . . . But wait. She must be around here, in this place. I can still feel her breath, in my face, in my nose. I go and I smell and I search and I can't find her. It's as though the earth had swallowed her."

"No, the earth has not swallowed her, Brother Wolf. No, indeed, she is here," the fox said. "I have seen her with my own eyes."

"You've seen her?"

"Yes, I've seen her, and I even know where she is."

"And you won't tell me?" growled the wolf. "She is mine. My morsel you are tearing from my mouth!"

"Brother Wolf! Brother Wolf! Certainly it isn't the first time that we are sitting together in this forest. We meet each other every day. Has it ever happened that I tore your food from your mouth?" The fox was indignant.

"Why are you getting so angry, Friend Fox?" answered the wolf. "It's only because of my great heartache and sorrow that I spoke as I did. But now, tell me, please, where did you see her?"

"In the little house."

"The one in the middle of the forest? In that house? I heard, Fox, that that little house in the forest is a very dangerous place. They say—"

"Oh, Brother Wolf, don't believe what they say. Only the foolish ones believe every lie they hear. But the clever one—his eyes are in his head. Come, let us go. I will show you the house and you will see for yourself and be convinced that Yemima is hiding from you. But, Friend Wolf, you won't forget me when you get that little prize? My children are also very hungry."

"And there's no danger in this thing? I'm afraid I will fall upon

8

some evil! My heart tells me—everyone is saying—this house is a place of danger."

"Oh, Wolf, my dear brother! And where is there a place absolutely safe and secure for us? What don't we do in order to live? A living, brother, everyone needs to make a living."

"True, true, Brother Fox."

And talking this way, they came to the house and stopped.

"Bend your ear and listen," whispered the fox into the wolf's ear. "Come nearer and listen. What do you hear?"

"Footsteps. I hear the sound of footsteps."

"Yemima's footsteps. She is waiting for her father to come and get her."

"How does one enter? The door is shut."

"Nothing easier. A little push with the head, my dear Wolf—a push of the door and it opens by itself."

"There is no difficulty at all?"

"Just a slight push of the door, Brother Wolf."

"And there is no—"

"Nonsense! If you're afraid, give me the girl and let me go in—but then she will be all mine! He is afraid," he said, to no one in particular. "A wolf afraid! Who ever heard of such a thing?"

"Just a little push?"

"A push—very slight, with the head in the door."

The wolf pushed with his head, and the door opened. In jumped the wolf. The door closed behind him and shut tight.

"There—lots of luck to you and all the best," cried the fox after him with a great laugh. "And this, my dear Wolf, is for all the things you have done to me—for the geese you robbed me of, for the little rabbit you tore from my mouth this past winter—for all the things you have stolen from me without pity. Now I have avenged myself. Yemima, my friend, is in my house, in my den. I have rescued her from your mouth for me and my little ones, who haven't had a taste of meat since the day before you robbed me of the rabbit."

And the fox ran quickly to his home, sweeping away the marks of his footsteps with his bushy tail.

All this time little Yemima was sitting with the little foxes, talking and having a good time. Her sharp ears had heard what the fox had whispered to his children, so she knew what was in store for her.

Yemima talked with the little foxes, told them stories, charmed them with her sweet voice, with her laughter and her little jokes. The little ones did not leave her for one minute, clinging to her, climbing all over her, on her knees, on her shoulders. She talked and talked, and all of a sudden she asked them, "What do you eat?"

"What do we eat? Nothing."

"Nothing? What kind of food is nothing?"

"Mice," they said. "We've been eating little mice. Since the Passover holidays we haven't tasted anything else—"

"And on Passover what did you eat?"

"On Passover? Daddy Fox brought us a roasted gosling from the big house on the other side of the river."

"Hmm . . . from the house on the other side of the river—and today?"

"From that day until today we've eaten only mice. Mama Fox hunts them and brings them to us. Daddy doesn't hunt mice."

"Have you ever eaten little roasted chickens?" Yemima asked.

"No. We've never in our lives tasted them and have never even seen them with our eyes."

"Little roasted chickens are very sweet, little foxes. Roasted chicken is a wonderful food—there is nothing better," cried Yemima. "Little

The little ones did not leave her for one minute . . .

roasted chickens are sweeter than honey. In my house, that big house on the hill, across the river, there are many, many roasted chickens! Wait for me here, little foxes, and I will run to the house and get some —I will bring you many, many roasted chickens, and you will eat them and be satisfied, and you will bless me. Because I like you very much, and I am very sorry for you, my little foxes."

The foxes were delighted, and Yemima jumped up and was off.

Happy and feeling good, the fox ran back to his den—but no Yemima! "Where is the girl I brought you this morning?" he demanded.

"Papa Fox! Papa Fox!" They jumped up on their little feet and began to talk all at once as they came dancing toward their father, swishing their tails with great joy. "The girl you brought us this morning is a very, very good girl. She heard that all we'd had to eat were the little mice. She was so sorry for us she went home to her house across the river, the house on the hill. Her mother has many little roasted chickens, and she went to get some and bring them to us. She said, 'Wait for me here, and I will run to the house and get some—I will bring you many, many roasted chickens. Little roasted chickens are sweeter than honey.' "

"Oh, stupid, stupid children!" cried the fox, and his eyes filled with tears. "Oh, my foolish little ones! How sly they are, the humans! Even their babies are as full of deceit as a pomegranate is full of seeds! And now, come, let us go from here. Let us flee, little foxes, lest this clever little girl does us even more harm."

In the house on the hill there was confusion and disorder. The father was running hither and thither; Dvora, the maid, was nervous and frightened; the mother had collapsed and was lying in a dead faint, and the old grandma was weeping and lamenting and wringing her hands. "Woe is us! Mima is gone! The little one has been killed!"

The sun had begun to set, and there was Yemima, walking and skipping and jumping up the hill, stumbling and falling over her long nightdress. She shouted from afar, "Papa! Mama! Grandma!"

And the girl threw herself on her father, mother, and grandmother and laughed through her tears as she told them all the things that had happened to her from the morning until the evening.

The very next day they went to the forest and killed the wolf, but the fox was gone. He, too, is clever.

How Sly-Fox
Was Fooled

◄§ SLY-FOX WAS THAT SAME FOX WHO HAD WANTED TO DEVOUR YEMIMA. When she escaped from him and ran home to her parents, the fox feared they would find out where he lived, so he left his cave in the great forest that same night and went off to a small grove and settled there, together with his wife and their cubs. He said to himself, "In this grove lived my parents and their parents before them. They supported themselves and their families. I, too, will support myself as they did."

So the fox lived there but found no livelihood. The small animals had become wise; all the fowl, even the stupid chickens, were now wise, and the foolish rabbits, too, slipped away from him. The mice, also, became very clever, and it was hard for him to catch even the little ones.

Every day Sly-Fox went out to seek his prey, but he found none. All day he walked around in the woods, crossed all the roads, stalked all the paths, and in the evening returned home as empty-handed as he had left.

His wife, Mrs. Sly-Fox, became angry with him and said, "Here, you are my husband, the father of our children. You are responsible for our support. Why don't you bring us food?"

14

So Sly-Fox decided he would no longer look for new ways to seek his prey, but would do what his ancestors had done. They had worked and were successful; he would do the same.

The fox went off, thinking his thoughts. Soon he saw a raven standing on a tree, with a piece of meat in his mouth. Stealthily he walked over to the tree and, keeping an eye on the raven's beak, spoke gently to him. "Oh, my Raven, how beautiful you are! Your feathers are like sapphire, your face is shining, and your voice is surely pleasant and sweet. Let me hear, I pray you, one of your best songs, and you shall rule over all the winged creatures on the earth and below the heavens."

The raven swallowed the piece of meat and then began to call, "Caw, caw, caw!"

The fox ran away in embarrassment and shame. The trick of his forefathers had not succeeded. His scheme did not work.

He was very hungry; the day was still long, and the sun stood in the middle of the sky. It was not time to return home. He walked and walked, and soon he saw a wide, shining lake. The fox walked up to the lake and saw in its clear water groups of bewildered fish, swimming with great caution, for there were many fishing boats on the water, and in the boats sat people who cast nets into the water, and on the banks of the lake sat fishermen with fishing rods. Sly-Fox thought, People are catching fish. I, too, will catch three or four fish now.

But how does one catch fish?

Very simple: grab them! Groups of fish were swimming close to the shore where he stood. He would put his paws in and grab!

He did indeed grab the fish in his paw, but in a second it was gone! It slipped out of his paw, swam calmly away in the lake, and in his paw there was nothing.

But people caught them and pulled them out.

Sly-Fox began to observe carefully what the fishermen were doing, and he saw:

People stood on the bank of the lake with poles in their hands. At the end of the poles was a string, and at the end of the string, on a hook, there hung a small worm. The fish saw the worm, rushed to it, and swallowed it. They swallowed it and were caught.

Thought the fox, A hook I don't have, but hairs in my tail I have. Perhaps I can make the fish think the hairs in my tail are worms.

So the fox turned to face the grove, with his back toward the lake. He put his tail into the water and moved and shifted its hairs, each hair

৶§ *He put his tail into the water . . .*

16

separately, hoping the fish would think they were worms. Thus he stood and waited and waited. In vain did he soak his tail in the water; not a single fish came up, not even the smallest of them. Even the most foolish was not fooled and did not approach his tail.

So Sly-Fox turned to the lake and watched the fish hurrying and slithering into the nets and saw some disappearing through the holes. Again he recalled what his ancestors had done, and he thought, I'll try one more thing. Maybe I'll succeed. Didn't my ancestors succeed?

He climbed up and stood on a rock, on the bank of the lake, and spoke to the fish. He made his voice sound pleasant and friendly. He did not speak, he chanted.

"Fish, my Fish, tell me, dear ones, why are you hurrying and rushing without any rest? Have you heard an alarm? Or have night robbers come upon you, armed bandits, that you are all running off to hide?"

Answered the fish: "And do you not see with your own eyes the nets and the traps? Men are planning to destroy us, us and our children."

Said Sly-Fox with great compassion, "I see your trouble, and my soul is sad within me. This is my only advice—it is good, it will work. In the grove there is my cave—I have just come from there. The cave is invisible, hidden from all eyes, and now it is empty and open. Come out and live with me, as your ancestors lived with mine."

Before Sly-Fox could finish his speech, Dagon, the dolphin, rose to the surface of the lake and said with equal compassion, "Your face does not look too good, my dear Fox—it has lost its glamour and majesty. I see your face today, and it looks as though you had been fasting. It seems that you are in pain, that your enemies are many. You should listen to *my* advice: come to live with me! I have room in the water's depths, invisible and hidden from all eyes. Live with us as your ancestors lived with . . . Oh, why are you running away? Has your heart fainted within you?" called Dagon. "Stop a minute, stop, stop! I have regards for you from that little girl, Yemima."

Ashamed and embarrassed, the fox stopped to rest deep, deep in the grove, very sad at heart. Suddenly he heard a whistling, and he turned to where the whistling came from, and saw, standing on a little hill, Rabbit, the Master-Magician, on his long hind legs, standing and shivering, trembling, his long ears erect, his eyes bulging with fear, staring at Sly-Fox.

Master-Magician was an old acquaintance of Sly-Fox. And Sly-Fox knew that Master-Magician had a wife, young and tender, white and clean, and she had three sons, little rabbits, fat and jolly, and five little daughters, plump and quiet. Master-Magician himself was very old, thin and dried out, without even a drop of flesh on him, a heap of dry bones, but he was better than nothing. The fox decided he would strangle him and drag him to his cave. It's better to gnaw the bones of a rabbit than to die of hunger, he thought.

No sooner said than done: Sly-Fox stole up to him from behind, slowly, slowly, and he was about to jump on Master-Magician and choke him when the rabbit gave a hoarse whistle.

"Sly-Fox, glorious Majesty! My old friend! Hear my voice and listen to me. We're in trouble, my children and my dear wife! I went out today in search of food and found a head of cabbage lying there in the bush. I even found two or three carrots lying near the big rock. So I got up on this hill and called my wife and children to come here. I whistled and whistled and there was no answer, because I had caught a cold and my voice couldn't be heard far. Won't you please stand in my place on this hill and whistle for them? But try to imitate my voice and they'll all come here together—my wife, whom I love, my sons and

Rabbit, the Master-Magician, his long ears erect . . .

my daughters, and perhaps my widowed sister will come too, the one who lives in my house.''

The fox heard this and his heart leaped with joy. He saw in his imagination the big fat mother rabbit, her little jolly sons and her plump quiet daughters, and maybe he would get in addition the old one's sister, the widow.

"Hurry, get off the hill and let me get on, and I will imitate your voice," called the fox.

The rabbit leaped off the hill and disappeared.

The fox whistled, raised his voice, but no one came—nobody.

Aryeh-Ben-Gadi and Fox-of-the-Burnt-Tail

A STORY FROM THE REIGN
OF THE JUDGES

◄§ MANY, MANY YEARS AGO, IN THE EARLY DAYS OF THE REIGN OF THE Judges (they ruled the people before there were Kings), there were not many people in the land of Israel, and large numbers of wild animals roamed the countryside.

Between Tzala and Estaol, cities in the land of Dan, there was an especially great number of lions and foxes. The lions would attack the herds of cattle and create confusion among them, and the foxes would steal into the chicken coops and pigeon houses and kill everything in them. The people of Dan and Judah would come out with their bows and arrows, spread their nets, and set traps, but it was no use. The animals grew and multiplied, and the land was filled with them.

When Shimshon, son of Manoah, grew up, he helped rid the land of many of the animals. He was unusually strong and clever and a very skillful hunter. His strength and cunning helped destroy the lions and chase the foxes away from the land.

One of the tricks Shimshon used was this: He would take a goat or lamb and tie it by its horns to a branch in a thicket or between the bushes where the lions were wont to pass. He would sit in ambush, with

◆§ The animals grew and multiplied, and the land was filled with them . . . .

bow and arrow in his hands, waiting and watching. The goat would
bleat or the lamb cry, and the lions would leap out of their hiding
places, ready to fall upon it. At that moment the sharp arrows of
Shimshon would fly out, piercing the lions and killing them. By means
of this trick Shimshon destroyed many lions, and the animals, realizing
the danger that lay in wait for them, stopped coming to the groves and
the bushes. The parents of the young lions would warn them, "Don't go
among the shrubs, and never rush in when you hear the voices of the

lambs or the bleating of the goats, for that will be your end.''

In one of the large caves outside the city of Tsarah in Dan, there lived a killer lion, big and very terrible, with his wife, the lioness, who was also big and a killer like her husband. They had a cub, who was beautiful and strong but not very smart. The lion was hungry, the lioness was hungry, and their cub was very hungry indeed. Every day the father lion would go out and hunt for food for his wife and son, and every evening he would return as empty-handed as when he had left.

All this time Shimshon, carrying his bow and arrows, would walk from pasture to pasture where the cattle were grazing. The animals feared him very much. The scent of his footsteps would throw terror into their hearts, and they would flee and hide in their caves.

The lions' hunger grew great, and one day the lioness jumped up, roaring and furious, and said to her husband, "Even though I am only

The parents of the young lions would warn them, "Don't go among the shrubs . . ."

the lioness and you are the lion, I will go and search for food, and I will bring food both for you and for our son. You are not a lion—you're a goat."

Thus spoke the lioness. She left the cave and walked right in among the bushes, following the bleating of the goat. But she never came back to her cave because Shimshon's sharp arrow had pierced her heart.

When this became known to the lions, they called the big one Baal-Gad, which means "the husband of the lioness who was killed by means of a goat," and the young cub they called Ben-Gadi, "the son of a lioness who fell because of a goat." The lion was enraged at this and vowed to attack Shimshon and kill him and thus restore his honorable name among the lions.

For three days and three nights the lion watched for Shimshon on the road that goes to Timnah. The lion knew that Shimshon would pass along the road, because he had been studying his habits for many days. Indeed, when Shimshon appeared, the lion leaped at him with a great roar to cast fear upon his heart, but Shimshon seized him by his beard and tore him apart, as he would a goat, and in his hand there was no weapon, neither sword nor spear.

When the news reached the lions, they called to the young cub, Aryeh-ben-Gadi, and said, "Your mother was killed by means of a goat, and your father was torn apart like a goat."

There also lived in this land a fox who was called Fox-of-the-Burnt-Tail. Some time before this, Shimshon had tied together the tails of three hundred foxes and had sent them off against the Philistines with fiery torches set into the midst of them. Many of those foxes were consumed by the fire, others were killed by the Philistines, and many were lost and no fox knows where they are. This one fox, although he, too, was not very smart, escaped and was saved from the fire, but his full and bushy tail was burnt and he had no hairs left on it, not even enough to sweep away his footsteps. That is why all his whereabouts and all his activities were known and everyone called him Fox-of-the-Burnt-Tail.

One day Aryeh-ben-Gadi and Fox-of-the-Burnt-Tail happened to meet and found favor in each other's eyes. They realized they were brothers in sorrow and had suffered the same sad lot. That day they talked things over and decided to leave the land of Dan and go elsewhere to live, to a more secure place where there would be no Shimshon and no lions and foxes who knew them and the events that caused them to be called by names of shame and disgrace.

They made an agreement. The lion would kill cattle and sheep and also man, whenever possible, and the fox would rob the chicken coops and the pigeon houses and perhaps would kill a little goat or a lamb when the opportunity arose. The lion would help the fox with his great strength and would support him in time of danger. The fox, on his side, would guide the lion with wise counsel and teach him ways of trickery. After they discussed all this and swore loyalty to each other (while each secretly decided to look out for himself only), they arose one evening and went to the mountainous land of Ephraim, far from the land of Dan.

It was the time of the harvest. Early in the morning the people of Tlulith, a village perched on a rock in the hills of Ephraim, went down to the valley, young and old, each one holding a scythe and a sickle. In the village only the old women were left to watch over the little ones. It was still dark, and the whole rock was enveloped in a gray fog, and silence reigned all around.

At that time Aryeh-ben-Gadi and Fox-of-the-Burnt-Tail quietly entered the village. They walked stealthily, carefully, step by step. When they came to the end of the village, they stopped under a window of a little house. Through the shutters a light from a small candle was seen shining, and the hoarse voice of a shrewd old woman named Pooah was heard as she was rocking the cradle of her little grandson and singing him a lullaby. The child was crying because he missed his mother, who was working in the field with her husband and the older sons. Pooah was rocking the cradle with all her might and singing a lullaby to the child. She was very tired and full of sleep, but the little one didn't let her rest.

> *"Sleep, sleep, my little one,*
> *My little one, my little one.*
> *Under the crib of my little son*
> *There stands a goat, an all-white one,*
> *From Ein-Gadi, from Ein-Gadi."*

"Do you hear?" whispered the fox to the lion. "Do you hear? She said, 'stands a goat.'"

> *"To the Jordan the goat will go.*
> *The goat will go—"*

"Perhaps we should go and watch for him on the road," said the lion. "Why should I stand here, in this dangerous place? Why should I risk my life and burst into the house? Perhaps even here, even in this house, Shimshon is hiding, sitting and waiting for us, ready to pounce on us from his hiding place. No," he said, "the best thing for me is to stand here outside on the road and watch for the white goat."

"Sh—sh," whispered the fox. "Wait, let's hear the end of the thing, and then we'll know what to do. Who knows? Perhaps for me and for you some food will be found here—for the two of us—for both of us."

Pooah was rocking the cradle with all her might . . .

The animals stood there, waiting, their ears perked and their hearts full of fear and hope. For two days and two nights they hadn't had a bit of food in their mouths. And the old woman was rocking the cradle and singing:

> *"Under the crib of my little son*
> *Stands a goat, an all-white one*
> *From Ein-Gadi, from Ein-Gadi.*
> *To the Jordan the goat will go.*
> *Figs so golden,*
> *Carob so sweet,*
> *The goat will bring, will bring to me*
> *From Ein-Gadi, from Ein-Gadi*
> *For my little one.*
> *My little one, sleep."*

It was quiet. In the sky there moved and floated a beautiful moon, and little stars were sparkling. A cool breeze was blowing. The trees in the small garden rustled. A sleepy brook bubbled quietly in the shelter of the rock. Silence.

"Fox, Fox," breathed the lion. "Do you know the road to the Jordan? You heard, 'the goat will go . . .' " But before he could finish, again the sound of the child's crying was heard and the voice of Pooah singing:

> *"If you don't sleep, my child, at all,*
> *For the lion I will call."*

"Hurray, hurray," growled the lion, "that is—"

"Sh," whispered the fox into his ear, all atremble. "In your hurry and carelessness you will spoil the whole thing. Quiet! Don't let your growls be heard. Hush."

The child was still crying. The old woman got down from her bed, went and sat near the crib and began to rock it, yawning and rubbing her eyes. The old one was getting angry, so she rocked the cradle hard and sang a frightening song:

"If you don't sleep, my son, at all,
To the lion I will call.
From the forests, from the woods
He will come to my child's bed.
Big and frightening yellow head,
He will listen to my song
And will carry you along
Far away, far away."

"Hurray!" said the lion. "Oh, but that's a clever old woman—yes, yes! 'Will carry you along.' "

"Will carry away my little one
Far away, my darling son.
He will come and he will take
My little one who's still awake.
Woe, oh, woe, oh, woe is me,
My little one, my little one."

The lion and the fox stood and listened, their hearts beating with joy, their mouths open and their eyes shining and burning like coals of fire.

"Listen, listen, dear Fox," said the lion. "Tell me, give me good counsel, for aren't you the clever one among all animals? You are a fox —a fox! Tell me, what am I to do now? Should I stand here and wait for the goat who went to the banks of the Jordan to bring back figs and carobs, or should I go to meet him? Or perhaps I should just break into the house, for there she is actually calling me, inviting me. Fox, dear Fox, what do you advise?"

The fox stood there, hesitating for a few minutes, listening, but to the lion he seemed lost in thought. After a while the cunning fox raised his head, turned to the lion, and with a soft, compassionate voice whispered into his ear, "Indeed, it does seem that Pooah is calling for help. And look at that child! There he is sleeping. His face is so pink and round, his hands, his legs—how chubby, how soft, how pure!"

The lion could contain himself no longer. "Hrrr!" he suddenly roared, and with his paw struck the door, which fell with a great noise and clatter. The lion stood on the threshold of the house.

The fox quietly disappeared and headed for the chicken coops. His sharp ears had caught the cry of a very young hen.

The lion stood on the threshold, thirsting for blood. His red eyes darted about, taking in the scene, and he stretched himself, ready to jump on his prey. But old Pooah, who had been sitting in a chair, half asleep and half awake, jumped up, frightened at the noise of the falling door. When she saw the fierce lion standing in the doorway, she ran to the cradle, stood protectively over the child, and cried, "Oh, my little one, my darling, don't be afraid! I will not give you to the lion, my child, don't fear." She continued to talk to him, soothing him, saying, "I will die in your stead, my darling. Don't worry, my star, my sun, my *shimshi*." The old woman did not know what magic was in the loving name *shimshi* (my sun) that she gave to her grandson.

Aryeh-ben-Gadi, who in the days of his youth had been terrified by the name Shimshon, thought Pooah was calling to that lion-killer and that he was hiding there somewhere in the room. He was terribly frightened.

"Hush, hush," called Aryeh-ben-Gadi, trembling with fear. "I have

30

The lion stood on the threshold, thirsting for blood . . . .

come in peace and you speak of war! Do not call for anybody. I didn't come to kill but to help. I am a lion of compassion."

Pooah stood at the cradle, looking at the lion and wondering at his words, but she didn't move. And Aryeh-ben-Gadi was speaking.

"I was walking by your house and heard your voice singing to the child. Sleep was overcoming you, and the child was crying and would not let you sleep. You were calling to some white goat, and the child was crying and crying, and then I heard you mention my name. You said:

'To the lion I will call.
From the forests, from the woods'

and so I came." He looked around nervously. "Of course I knew that only to frighten the child did you say those words. But I am not angry; I am not one of the angry kind. I am a good and forgiving lion," he said, a bit louder so that if Shimshon *were* listening, he would look on him more kindly. "Go and lie down till the morning and I, now that I'm here, I will rock the cradle for you, if you wish." The lion's words were soft, for he had made his voice gentle.

Pooah was very clever—as were all the women of Ephraim—clever and courageous, and she answered, "Listen to me, Lion! I believe in your sincerity and your good heart. I can see you are not like the rest of the lions. But, lord of the animals, you know that your large mane, your sharp teeth, and your great roar will frighten my grandchild. If you will allow me to muzzle your mouth, if you will allow me to bind your feet —that is, tie them to the leg of the cradle—then I will go and rest. You can rock the cradle, and the child will sleep. And as a reward when the morning comes, I will prepare a big feast from the white goat that is coming from Ein-Gadi—a good, soft goat. You will eat and be satisfied, and in peace I will send you off."

"Perhaps there is some food now?" asked the lion hopefully.

"No, my lord Lion, I have nothing here in the house. There was the white goat," Pooah said, "but I sent him to the Jordan to bring back figs and carobs. He will be back very soon, and you will eat him and feel good."

"Do what you think is best," said the lion, still thinking of Shimshon. "I trust you, you won't do me any evil because I came not to do bad but to help you."

Pooah took an iron bridle and muzzled the lion's mouth. Then she took a damp rope and tied his leg to the middle pillar, which supported the house, and said, "Strong lion! Rock the cradle of my grandchild, and I will give my eyes a little rest, for I'm very tired."

It wasn't very pleasant for the lion with the bridle in his mouth. He tried to pull the leg toward him, but the rope was very strong. He consoled himself with the thought, Once Pooah falls asleep, I will gnaw the bridle, untie the rope, and make myself a wonderful feast with the child. But then another thought struck him. Suppose he couldn't gnaw the bridle? Suppose he couldn't untie the rope? Then the goat would return from the Jordan, and the fox, the burnt-tailed one, would be watching for it and would kill it—that thief, that yellow swindler! A shiver went through the lion, and he called out to the old woman, "Pooah! Hey, Pooah!"

"What do you wish, my great Lion?" Pooah asked as she turned to him.

"Pooah, my dear! I confess to you that I did not come here alone, but together with that yellow thief, the fox of the burnt tail. That evil one persuaded me to come here, for he said, 'It is harvest time now for the people of Tlulith, and before the sun comes out, they will go to the valley to harvest the wheat, and only the old ones and the children will remain. Let us go there and we will divide our prey. You,' said the scoundrel to me, 'you will kill Pooah, the old woman, first, and then you will eat the little one for dessert and I will go to the coops.' That's what he said to me. But, Pooah," he continued, "I am a lion, the king of the forest. I will say to the burnt-tailed one, 'In the land where my father ruled, one didn't do such things. One doesn't attack a weak old woman or an innocent child. I will be fair, and with clean hands I will find my prey, and now . . .' "

Before he could finish speaking, there arose such a noise! The birds called, the roosters crowed, the chickens cackled, the doves cooed, the geese and the goslings honked! Old Pooah trembled, and, jumping up, she grabbed the rake in one hand and the tent peg in the other and ran to the yard of the fowls.

And she saw the fox crouching near the coop, ready to leap out at the birds. He was carefully eyeing the biggest of the hens and the fattest. The old woman went quietly behind him, and with the rake she gave him a blow on his back.

The fox winced at the pain. His eyes filled with tears, and he turned to her and cried in a pleading voice, "Pooah, my Pooah! Why are you hitting me—I, who am your sincere admirer? I came here only to *warn* them and to save them from the lion who is here, preying on them, for he was planning to kill all your birds in one morning. That's why I came —to warn these stupid creatures. I wanted to tell them not to crow or cackle or call, and then I wanted to come to you and tell you about the lion. You don't know him, but he, Ben-Gadi—he kills goats and lambs."

34

You are clever, my fox, thought the old woman to herself, but I, too, wasn't born yesterday. She said in a soft voice, "Pardon me, dear Fox. I've gotten old, and my brain has gotten weak from age. But in vain do you speak evil of the lion; he is really very fair and just. At this very moment he is standing and rocking my grandchild's cradle, and if it weren't for the terror of the birds at the appearance of an evil fox—excuse me—but there are some among your brethren—"

"There are, there are, to my great sorrow! There are indeed deceivers and swindlers among my people," answered the fox, shaking his head sadly.

"You see," said Pooah, "you admit it yourself that there are bad foxes! If I weren't afraid of them, I would be sleeping now. All night I haven't slept."

"Pooah, Pooah dear! Go and give some sleep to your eyes. I will watch your birds—don't worry, don't be afraid."

"Blessings on your head," said Pooah, "but forgive me, please, for I am a foolish woman and a very timid one. I am still afraid of you, but if—if you allowed me—I would take a thin rope and tie your leg or your tail to the tree, to that dried-out carob tree standing in the yard in front of you. Then I would be able to lie down in peace, and my heart would not tremble."

"Hmm, hmm," said the fox, "I don't mind if you tie me up. But the results might prove bad for you, not for me. Suppose a wicked fox comes stealing in or an eagle swoops down on your birds, and I, the watchman, am tied and bound?"

"You are right, my clever one, you are right," said Pooah. "Not with a short rope will I tie you, but with a long one so you will be able to walk the length and breadth of the yard as though you weren't bound at all. You'll be able to walk among the birds like a general in his army."

35

"If that's what you will do," said the stupid fox, "then tie me up, by all means."

But Pooah took a short, thick rope and, standing behind him, she tied his leg and his tail securely to the carob tree, and said, "Good-bye and all the best to you. Watch well, my dear, watch well. Tomorrow morning I will prepare for you a fine feast from the white goat that went to the Jordan."

And thus the dawn broke. The eastern sky reddened, and over the hills of Ephraim the sun began to rise and light up the earth. The stars faded, one after the other, and the moon became paler and paler until it was just a white spot in the heavens. From the valley the harvesters were coming, and everywhere the windows were being opened.

Old Pooah was standing at her door, a smile on her wrinkled face. She waved to her children who were returning from the fields to have some breakfast and to sleep for a few hours. When the sun went down in the late afternoon, they would return to their work.

She waved to them from afar and called, "Hurry! Hurry! We have guests, very important guests."

And when they came, she showed them the two "guests"—Aryeh-ben-Gadi and Fox-of-the-Burnt-Tail—tied and bound.

The Diamond

OUTSIDE THE SNOW IS FALLING—SOFT, WHITE SNOW. THE SUN IS SETTING —there is still some light, but in the little house it is dark, dark and cold because its only window is frozen and covered with ice.

A mother and her children are standing at this window. They want to look out and see what is happening, who is coming and who is going. Even though they are not expecting anyone, they want to watch the people in the street.

The mother blows on the windowpane. It is a long time before she clears one little spot, the size of a small coin. She picks up her little daughter in her arms, and the two big boys stand on their toes and they all look out on the street.

And they see: fathers, older brothers and sisters returning home, some from work, some from school—all walking happily because they will soon see their children or their little brothers or sisters; mothers are coming from stores carrying food. Only their father is not coming— their father is dead, and the mother stands desolate and alone.

Outside snow is falling, soft white snow. Children, well-fed, dressed in warm clothing, are sliding on the snow, throwing snowballs, laugh-

A mother and her children are standing at the window . . . .

ing, shrieking, running, hurrying, and playing—their voices ring joyfully. Only her children, ragged and barefoot, are standing in the small
dark house, in her empty home.

And the mother is saying to herself, "God, you have so much light
and warmth, bread and milk and wood for all—have you nothing at all
for me and for my poor children?"

And one tear from her eye falls upon the windowpane.

Outside the snow is falling—white, soft snow. Fathers are walking
happily, mothers are returning joyfully from stores, laden with all
kinds of good things to eat. And everyone is stopping in front of the
little house to look at the windowpane, gazing and wondering.

On the window, on the frozen pane, there, where the mother had
cleared the tiny spot with her breath, her tear glistens like a diamond,
shining seven times brighter than light, like the color of gold and
silver. And the tear is more beautiful than the precious stone in a king's
crown and more beautiful than the brightest star that shines in the
sky.

A very rich man pushes his way through the crowd, opens the door,
and says, "I will give you much money and you will have plenty of food
for yourself and your children. Please give me the diamond that is on
your window."

"That is not a diamond," she answers, "not even a precious stone. It
is a bitter tear from the eye of a mother."

Again the door opens, and an even richer man enters. He approaches
the woman and says, "I will give you a big house with seventy-seven
rooms and pillars of marble. You will drink from glasses of gold, and
you will eat from silver plates. Only give me the diamond that is on your
window."

39

"That is not a diamond," she replies, "not even a precious stone. It is a bitter tear from the eye of a mother."

The door opens a third time, and in comes the king himself, with a golden crown upon his head and a silver sword hanging at his side.

"Take from me my crown and take my great silver sword, but give me that jewel," the king says.

The mother says, "I don't want your crown of gold, nor do I want your great silver sword—but take for yourself the jewel, if you can."

The king goes over to the window. He wants to take the jewel, but it is dancing, slipping from between his fingers, and he cannot touch it and cannot grasp it. In his anger he strikes at the jewel and cracks the window.

Outside the snow is falling—soft, white snow. All are sleeping in their warm homes, lying in their beds under warm covers—sleeping, contented and happy, and dreaming pleasant dreams. But in the little house it is dark and cold and desolate.

A cold draft is blowing through the broken window; the children are trembling with cold and crying out in their sleep, and the mother is standing at the window, thinking, Dear God, you have given your creatures so many things—bread and milk and all kinds of food. You have given them gold and silver and crowns of gold—why didn't you also give them good hearts?

And tears are falling from her eyes, one tear after another, and the cold wind carries them, these tears, and changes them to precious stones and shining pearls, and the little house becomes filled with many jewels that are dancing and flying around.

The door opens and an old man comes in. His beard is long, long and white, white like pure silver.

40

And with his entrance the jewels disappear and the house becomes filled with light and warmth. In the oven there is a fire burning brightly, and it is filled with pots and pans, and in them wonderful foods are cooking and giving forth a mouth-watering aroma.

Around the table the children are sitting, dressed in warm clothing, new and lovely. They are eating the good food, and their cheeks are pink, and their eyes are shining like precious jewels.

The mother is standing before the old man, standing and looking at him, and she says, "I had one beautiful diamond, and the king wanted it. Before you came, my house was filled with many precious stones, and they've all disappeared. I would have given them to you, dear, good old man."

"I have it all, even the diamond the king wanted."

The mother wants to talk with him, to ask the old man questions, to consult with him—and . . .

The old man is not here, he has vanished, the good old man, and is gone.

The Good Sons

✑ ONCE UPON A TIME THERE WAS A KING AND A QUEEN WHO WERE VERY unhappy because they had no children. The king especially was more despondent than any other childless person. He wanted to have a son who would inherit his great kingdom. Such a son, he thought, would sit on his throne after him and would commemorate his name after his death.

The king and queen consulted doctors, sages, and sorcerers. They also sought the advice of the great men of God. But it was all in vain. The king and queen had no son.

The queen was sad. The king became more and more despondent, and when he was alone, he wept a great deal. Thus passed many days.

One day he went out to battle against a king from another land. He gathered all the good strong young men of his kingdom and forced them into his army.

There was a great outcry: the mothers wept, the fathers lamented, the brides wailed, the young women and their children screamed and moaned and tore their clothes.

But what could one do? The king had declared war and everyone was obliged to go and fight.

On the day that the young men were to leave for war, there came to the king an old man, who bowed before him and said, "My lord King, it is well known that all your life you have been unhappy because God has not given you a son who would bear your name after your death. You have consulted doctors, sages, sorcerers, and great men of God—to no avail. But if you will follow *my* advice and do what I tell you, you will have a son whose name will be great in the land and who will bring you great honor."

The king rejoiced at the words of the old man and said, "Whatever you tell me I will do. And if what you say is true, I will give you beautiful gifts, even half my kingdom!"

The old man shook his head. "I have no desire for your gifts and no need for kingdoms. Only do what I tell you. All the young men whom you had planned to send to war to kill and to ravage must return, each to his father's house or to his wife and children. Order them to break their swords and return to their work in the fields or in the forests. If you will do this, you will have a son."

On that very day all the soldiers returned with joy and with song to their homes.

Mothers and wives blessed the king; fathers sang his praises.

A year went by, two years, three years—but the king and queen had no son. The king sent for the old man and said, "You told me that a son would be born to us if I didn't go to war. I listened to you. Yet we still have no son."

The old man was surprised. "You still do not have a son, my lord King? And I surely thought the king would have a son by now! Well,

&"If you will follow my advice, you will have a son . . ."

then, if you will do what I suggest now, you will have a son the likes of which no other king in all the world ever had.

"In this great kingdom of yours there are many, many thousands of people who cannot read or write because they have no place to study and no one to teach them. Order houses to be built for them, beautiful schools with good teachers to teach them. Then you will have a wonderful son."

The king did as he was told. His land became filled with schools, and everywhere was heard the sound of children's voices studying and reciting. The king's praises were sung over the whole land. The people blessed his name.

A year passed, two years, three years passed—still the king and queen had no son. Once again the king sent for the old man and said to him, "You promised me that if I did what you told me to do we would have a son. Where is he?"

"You still have no son?" asked the old one. "And I thought surely you would have a son by now! Well, just do as I tell you now, and you will have a son whose name will be known from one end of the earth to the other.

"In your land there are many mountains and valleys, and buried in them are gold and silver and iron. All these good things belong to a few rich people who do not work themselves, while thousands of people work hard for them and do not have enough food to eat or clothing to wear.

"Divide this land equally among your people so that no one will have more than his neighbor. Then there will be no envy and no hatred in the world. If you will do this, you will have a son who will be the greatest of all men."

The king did what the old man told him to do. The people of his land were very happy. The fields were covered with grass and with all kinds of grain; the gardens and the forests were filled with fruit trees. The land was free of hatred and envy. The king was loved by all, his name was praised, and he was given great honor.

A year passed, two years, three years, many years went by. The king grew old, the queen grew old, and still there was no son.

One day as the king was sitting on his throne, the old man appeared, bowed before him, and said, "My lord, how are your sons? Are you pleased with them? Do you also remember to bless my name?"

The king became angry and said to him, "You know I have no sons, and yet you come to mock me?"

"Heaven forbid that I should mock you!" said the old man. "But you have three good sons who will give honor to your name, and as long as your land exists your name will be remembered. Your oldest is named Peace, your second one is called Knowledge, and the third son's name is Justice. What king in the world has sons as good as these?"

The king looked at the old man tenderly and said, "You are right, old one. We are happy with our sons."

Flying Money

⟡ ONCE UPON A TIME IN A SMALL VILLAGE THERE LIVED A BROTHER AND a sister. The brother's name was Merori ben Tsur, (Merori, son of Tsur), and the sister's name was Naama. The brother was fifteen years old when Naama was born, at a time when Tsur and his wife were elderly, and so Naama was the child of their old age. They were well-to-do people, owners of estates and vineyards, where many servants worked. Merori grew to manhood, married, and lived with his wife in his father's house, worked the fields as though they were his own, and his diligence gave his parents much joy, for he was the elder and the only son.

When their time drew near, the parents summoned Merori and said, "We are about to go the way of all on earth, and there is no one above you in the house, for you are the older one. Therefore you shall remain upon the land of your ancestors, and Naama, your sister, shall live with you until she grows up. You shall bring her up and educate her like a daughter. When the time comes for her to wed, you shall see that she marries a decent and righteous man who will be good to her, and you shall give her a share of the inheritance of your father, according to the law. And you shall let her enjoy all the goods with which the Lord has blessed you, for you are her older brother, and it shall be well with you and with her forever."

The old people blessed their son and daughter, closed their eyes, and died.

Merori was a hard, deceitful man who loved money. When the period of mourning for his parents was over, he summoned two wanton, worthless men and showed them a will he himself had written, which stated that all the land and estates had been left to him and that his sister, Naama, got nothing at all. He gave the false witnesses some money and they signed the will, stating that it had been drawn up in their presence. Then Merori and the two witnesses came to the Elders at the gate and showed them the will, written and sealed. And the witnesses testified before the Elders and all the people.

All were amazed that the father had left everything to his son and nothing to his daughter, but what was done was done, and no one can change a will written and signed before witnesses.

As soon as Naama reached womanhood, Merori put her out of the house and gave her nothing of her father's inheritance. Naama went to work in the homes and fields and vineyards of the village folk who had known her all her life. After some time one of the workers in the field fell in love with her. She loved him, too, and they were married. Together they worked in the fields. They built themselves a little house on the road at the end of the village, and there they lived modestly, but in peace and contentment. Naama bore him two sons and two daughters. Then the husband fell ill and, after being very sick for two or three weeks, he died. Naama was left a widow, a poor mother of four little children. But even then her brother had no pity for her and hardened his heart against her.

Naama continued to work in the fields and vineyards during the day, and at night cared for her children, washed and mended their clothes, and taught them to take care of one another during the day while she was away from home. Through all her poverty and misery Naama never refused a kindness to anyone who asked it of her, and her little house was always open to every passerby and wanderer, and every poor man found rest and food in her house.

But her rich brother was evil and hardhearted. His house was always locked, and in vain would a wanderer knock on his door, by day or night. He never gave a hungry man a piece of his bread, nor did he let any man cross his threshold.

One year on his birthday Merori gave a big party for the wealthy people of the village who were his friends and intimate companions. On the morning of that day Naama came to congratulate him, saying, "I've come to you, my brother, on your birthday, for I have just learned that you are having a big party this evening for all your acquaintances, and I, who am your flesh and blood, have not been invited. Don't deprive me of the pleasure of your blessing, for I've come to you on a day of celebration."

But Merori spoke harshly to her and said, "To you I shall give nothing, nothing from my house or from the food on my table which I have prepared for those who are greater and better than you!"

Naama left, embittered and insulted, with tears in her eyes.

Very late that night an old man passed through the village, walking bowed under a heavy sack on his back. The night was very dark, a heavy rain beat down on the land, and a strong wind was blowing. All the houses in the village were closed, their windows shuttered, and not a light showed through their cracks, for the hour was late and everyone was asleep. The old man stopped and looked around, and then he saw a big, spacious, well-lit house. Through the windows he could see happy

49

CENTRAL ARKANSAS LIBRARY SYSTEM
LITTLE ROCK PUBLIC LIBRARY
700 LOUISIANA
LITTLE ROCK, ARKANSAS

An old man passed through the village . . .

people seated at a table, eating and drinking and enjoying themselves. Their host was serving and entertaining them. The old man came to the door, knocked, and said loudly:

> "A poor old wanderer I,
> Weary and weak from the road.
> Please open the door, for I'm thirsty,
> Please open the door for I'm hungry,
> Please give me a place to sleep."

Out on the threshold came Merori, master of the house, and spoke
harshly to him:

"Not for the likes of you
Have I prepared my table.
Not for the likes of you
Have I roasted my meat.
Not for the likes of you
Have I brought out my wine.
Go away, you miserable pauper!
Take off, and get on your way!"

Merori spoke harshly to him . . .

Thus he spoke and slammed the door in his face. The old man sighed and turned and went off into the darkness of the night. He walked and walked, bent under his pack, drenched by the rain and shivering from the cold wind. He walked until he came to the house of Naama at the end of the village. He looked through the window and saw a candle burning on the table and a woman sitting and sewing. The old man went to the door, knocked, and called:

"A poor old wanderer am I,
Weary and weak from the road.
Please open the door for I'm thirsty,
Please open the door, for I'm hungry,
Please give me a place to sleep,
For miserable and weary am I."

Naama, sorry for the old man, opened the door and said:

"Come, come, blessed of the Lord.
My table is spread for you,
My water is pure for you,
Here is my bread for you,
Here is a bed for the weary.
Come into my house,
And you shall find peace."

The old man entered the house, removed his sack, put down his stick, and stretched out on the bench near the wall, for he was very tired. Naama, noticing that he was wet, hurried and gave him her husband's clothes. She made a fire, and when he had changed, she put the wet clothes near the stove to dry. Then she set the table and gave the man bread and soup, although it was the soup she had cooked for the next day for her children. The man satisfied his hunger and blessed the Lord. He thanked the woman for her kindness. Then she prepared a bed for him on the bench, the old man lay down, and she covered him with her blanket to keep him warm. Naama took the old man's torn and tattered clothes and sat down at the table and patched them, for she thought the old man was asleep.

But he was not sleeping; he merely pretended to be asleep. He looked at her from under the blanket and saw everything she did. Then his face began to shine, and from the light of his face the whole house filled with a great light, as though the dawn had come.

Naama looked bewildered and amazed: the night was still young, yet the house was full of light! She did not know that the old man was an

❧ *Naama took the old man's torn and tattered clothes and patched them . . .*

angel of the Lord, sent from above to see if the people were kind and
good to one another and to reward the pure of heart and the righteous
as they deserved.

In the morning the old man spoke to Naama and said, "The kindness
you have shown me God has seen. Behold, I give you this small coin,
worth only one penny, but there is a blessing in it. This coin will give
you all your heart desires if you do just this: at midnight, when all are
asleep and no one sees, shut the door in every room, place this coin on
the table, and say the words I shall put into your mouth. But beware
of asking too much! Do not rush to become rich, and ask only for what
you and your children need day by day. If you do this, it will go well
with you and your children all your days, and the day will come when
the coin will restore the inheritance your brother has stolen from you."

The man finished speaking and vanished. He flew off and was gone.

That very same night, at midnight, when footsteps were no longer
heard in the streets and all the villagers were asleep, and her children
were also asleep, each one in his place, and the house was very quiet,
Naama took the coin into her room and shut the door. She lit the
candle, placed the coin in front of her on the table, and whispered:

"Coin, coin, coin of mine,
Help me now in my great need!
Grant me my allotted bread
For this day, which I await.
Not too little, not too much,
But only that which I do need,
Without work, without toil.
Coin, coin, coin of mine,
Help me now in my great need."

54

&ᶘ *"Behold, I give you this small coin . . ."*

And the coin began to spin on the table, like the dreidel with which little children play. Thus it spun, turned in a circle, spun a minute or two longer, and stopped. And behold! Coins of silver and copper were scattered on the table.

Naama counted the coins and found a total of one dinar and twenty pennies. Not a penny was lacking for all the needs of her household for that day.

She was very happy and gave thanks to the Lord. From that day on she did this every night until the fifth day. The night before the sixth day, at midnight, Naama entered her room, shut the door, and, with a trembling heart, whispered to God. Then she took the coin, placed it in front of her on the table, saying:

> "Coin, coin, coin of mine,
> Help me now in my great need.
> Do not spoil the Sabbath day.
> Make the holy Sabbath pleasant,
> Make the holy Sabbath sweet.
> Not too little, not too much.
> For me this day of all is best,
> Because on this day God did rest."

And lo! The coin spun, spun seconds after seconds, minutes after minutes. It did not stop, and in its hurried spinning, nimble and dizzying, it scattered coins of silver, copper, even of gold.

Naama stood and gazed, her heart within her quickening, all her bones quivering, for she feared that she might have asked for too much and that this time the coin might bring forth a curse and not a blessing. She wanted to stop it, but could not, for the old man had not told her

Thus she stood, overwhelmed and bewildered . . .

how. Thus she stood, overwhelmed and bewildered, until the coin stopped, leaving a big pile of coins on the table.

When Naama counted the coins, she found a sum the like of which she had not seen since Merori had driven her out of her parents' house —seventy-five silver dinars and seventy-three copper pennies. She stood at the table as though rooted to the floor, looking at that big pile of money. Could that large sum be for the needs of just one Sabbath? She was greatly puzzled. She sat down and began to think, and she suddenly found the answer.

Yesterday and the day before, as she had been sitting contentedly at home with her children, she had seen that their clothes were shabby and torn from too much wear, and that their shoes were worn out. She looked at her own shoes—how patched they were! Patch upon patch, with no room for any more. She thought of the rainy days that were coming soon; neither she nor her children had warm jackets; it was already time to send the older boys to school, but there was no money, no help, and no one to lean on.

Now, as she sat on her chair and recalled this, she began to add up the cost of the clothes and the shoes, just simple things and not for show. She found that, coin for coin, it added up exactly to seventy-three dinars and nineteen copper pennies, and that for the needs of the Sabbath— two challas, candles, wine for kiddush, meat, fish, and other things for the Sabbath table—it added up to two dinars and fifty-four pennies—the right amount, as right as the day!

"Oh, coin, coin of mine, you did truly help me in my need!" Naama cried, and rose from her chair, feeling happy.

The following day Naama went to the stores and bought for herself and for the children cloaks and dresses, warm jackets for the coming rainy days, and new shoes. And she prepared the Sabbath with an open hand and with a carefree heart. She and her children had not had so good and complete a Sabbath since that good old man, the man of God, had appeared.

Days and weeks rushed by, and the months passed. Every midnight Naama whispered to the coin, and the coin worked and gave her everything she needed, never less, never more, than the expenses of her household.

During the rainy season, when the roof of her house leaked, and the windowpanes had to be replaced, and when she began to send her sons to school, the coin of its own accord added money for the roof, for the windowpanes, and for all their school needs. Then in the middle of the winter, when the time came for Puah, her daughter, to go to school, the coin gave of its own accord the tuition fee for the girl as well.

As for Naama, she did nothing but take care of her house and her children. Her bread was provided; all her needs were filled; she lacked nothing in the house. The children grew beautiful and healthy; she also was strong and beautiful, and everything went well. All the village people and all those who had known her during her days of poverty looked at her in amazement. Where was she getting all that? Who was it who supported her and provided for all her needs? They talked about her, gossiped, estimated the expenses of her household, conjectured all sorts of possibilities. No one knew anything definite—it was a puzzle.

During all that time, in the house of Merori, there was great confusion. The members of his household were at their wit's end, because he had changed; his behavior was strange. Every night at midnight, when everyone was asleep in bed dreaming their dreams, Merori would rise, go to his treasure room where he kept his money and his gold securely locked in trunks of iron and copper, and run around it, his face burning, his hands outstretched, crying loudly, "My coins are fluttering! My coins are flying! My coins are disappearing! They are lost!"

His sons, his daughters, his wife, and all his relatives saw nothing. Awakened from sleep, they tried to calm him. "They are vain visions, hallucinations. . . ." But he insisted. "Look, they're flying! Dinars of gold and silver—they flutter and disappear, vanish! Coins of copper, small pennies, fly away and are gone!"

After two or three minutes he didn't see the fluttering coins any more; sweat covered his entire body; he trembled. After resting awhile and becoming calm, he opened his treasure box, counted his daily bundle of coins, and found sums of money missing, small sums or large, but always there was something missing. His family argued with him and said he surely must have made a mistake in his reckoning, for no one had entered his room. There was no sign of forced entry, or even the slightest sign that anyone had touched anything or carried anything off or loitered even a single minute in his room, which was always locked. But he insisted that with his own eyes he saw his money fly out of the chest and disappear, and he could not stop it.

His family talked with him, his accountants went over his books and records and came up with all sorts of theories, but no one could say anything definite.

Naama knew nothing about what was being said about her in the village, and, of course, nothing of what was happening in her brother's house.

She was at ease and happy with the blessing of the man of God which hovered over her. He surely approved of what she was doing, for she followed his instructions and did everything he commanded. She had no desire to become rich, and did not ask for great things. She was satisfied with her lot.

ﻬ§ "My coins are fluttering! My coins are flying!"

The rainy season was over and spring was approaching. One clear day when the three older children were in school and the little girl was taking her afternoon nap, Naama was sitting by the bed. The sun was shining through the small window, lighting up the house, filling it with the joy of the coming spring, and Naama sat and thought, God is good and very dear to me. Great are the kindnesses which He has performed for me, but how long shall my life and the life of my children depend upon miracles? If I had a piece of land close to my house, I would plow it, seed it, and then I would support myself like other people, by the toil of my hands and the sweat of my brow. And when my children grew up, they could work with me in the field and in the garden, and I would no longer be dependent upon the miraculous kindness of God, but upon the great kindness He extends to all His creatures, daily, according to the ways of nature.

And then she thought, when the children grew into adults, who would inherit the coin? God forbid that she should do what her parents had done—leave everything to one and let the others be dependent upon him! Even if she left them the coin, how could it be divided? Besides, she was not even sure that the coin had been given to her forever and to her offspring after her.

Thus she sat and pondered all that day and the rest of the days that week. With these thoughts in mind, she began to walk around outside her house, appraising the fields. She noticed an unused village pasture behind her house, a field never worked before, virgin soil, without any owner. This field Naama desired.

The following week, one of the first days of spring, at midnight, Naama stood in her locked room, the coin on the table in front of her, and prayed in a whisper:

"Coin, coin, coin of mine,
Help me now in my great need.
When you give my daily bread,
When you give me all my needs,
Let it be through work and toil,
Not less, not more, just what I need.

Help me live
By the toil of my hands,
Help me eat
By the sweat of my brow.
Coin, coin, coin of mine,
Help me now in my great need!"

The coin began to spin in place, spinning and turning, one minute, two minutes, three, four, and coins of silver and gold were thrown, scattered all over the table, hundreds of them. Still the coin continued to spin while Naama stood and watched, her heart beating within her like a bird in a cage. When the coin stopped spinning, Naama sat and counted the dinars, the pennies, and all the coins—and behold! The sum total was four hundred dinars of silver, plus two dinars in small change for the needs of the next day. Then Naama knew that God had heard her prayer and that the money was given to her to buy the field she wanted.

The next day Naama went up to the gate and sat there. Zidkiyohu, the village Elder, was there, as were the other Elders, each sitting on his chair around him. Many people were there, standing or sitting at the gate, for it was a judgment day, when the people came with their problems to the judges.

When it was Naama's turn to come before the judge, she arose, approached him, and said that she intended to buy a piece of land for herself and for her children after her, and that she had in mind the abandoned pasture near her house at the end of the village, virgin land which the villagers were not using. The matter seemed good in the eyes of Zidkiyohu and in the eyes of his colleagues. They told her the price of the field, and it was the exact sum which the coin had thrown upon the table. Then Naama knew it was God's will that she should buy the field. She took out the bundle of money from her pocket, counted it into the hand of Zidkiyohu, dinar after dinar until the last dinar, in the presence of all the Elders. Then Zidkiyohu rose and said, "It is yours to buy!" and according to custom, he removed his shoe, indicating an agreement.

Naama then said to the Elders and to all the people, "You are witnesses this day that I have bought the field which is at the end of the village near my house, the field and all the trees on it, for myself and as inheritance for my children after me. You are witnesses this day."

Then the Elders rose and said within the hearing of all the people, "This piece of land at the end of the village adjoining the house of Naama, daughter of Tsur, is sold to her, bought by her for herself and for her children after her, forever!"

They wrote it down in a book, witnessed and sealed in a contract. And Zidkiyohu, the chief judge, blessed Naama in the hearing of all the people, and said, "Build your house for eternity, and walk in the path of righteousness as you have been doing, for everyone knows that you are a woman of valor. Command your children to follow the good path and walk on it after you. May the field give you enough bread for you and your children."

Then the people approached and blessed Naama, and she rose, bowed to them, and went home in good spirits.

64

There was one who stood apart at the gate, and when he saw what went on, he trembled with a great fear, his eyes bulging from their sockets, his face white as chalk. That was Merori, her brother. Now he understood that the coins he saw flying away every night in his room were not hallucinations, but real, for even last night at midnight his money had left his treasure chest, risen, and flown around the room until it disappeared from sight. And when this terrible vision had passed, he had counted his money and discovered that four hundred dinars were missing—the very dinars which Naama had counted out and placed into the hand of Zidkiyohu, the village Elder!

Angry and confused, Merori slipped away from the people and went home. What should he do? How could he go before the Elders and the people and tell them about these things? They wouldn't believe him! If his family considered him crazy, how could strangers believe him to be sane?

The people of this village had a custom: they would take seeds from their own fields and give them to the buyer of a new field, each one according to what his heart advised him. They also gave some shoots of olive trees and red vines for planting in the olive orchard and vineyard. And so they followed this custom for Naama.

Only Merori did not give anything, for his hand was shut tight and his heart was hard, and he always guarded his possessions.

When it was time to plow, Naama went to the field, measured a small part of it with a rope, and worked it by hand, for she still had no ox or mule for plowing. She worked the field with a hoe and an ax, and she did that in the garden, too. She sowed and planted whatever she had on hand, saying to herself, "Let God give me only the necessities—food for me and my household."

And the dew came down upon the planted piece of land and watered it. After some time the seeds sprouted, the land became green, and the garden began to bloom.

When the people in the area saw this, they were happy and said, "Naama's hands are blessed. God gives her good luck in everything she does."

At harvest time Naama went to the field, worked all day, and on the first day she bound five sheaves and set them up, side by side, in a single row. When she returned to the field the next morning, she saw another row standing alongside the first one. She counted the sheaves, there were five in the second row, ten sheaves altogether. Naama wondered greatly at this, her heart beating in fear. Thus it was on the second day, and on the third, and every day until the end of the harvest. Every morning she found double of what she had harvested.

The vintage days came, and again she found every morning double the number of bunches of grapes and olives. She was no longer surprised —she had had experience with miracles, and she said to herself, "That's the work of the coin which the man of God gave me. The kindness of God has not ended, His compassion is not finished. Blessed is He and blessed His great name."

The day came for the gathering of the crops, and Naama's children helped her. She filled the vessels, which the children carried away and then returned with the empty ones. Then she heard a voice greeting her, saying, "The Lord be with you, woman of valor."

Naama turned to the speaker and saw Zidkiyohu standing before her. She bowed to him and said, "God bless you, Zidkiyohu! What has brought my lord to his servant?"

He answered her and said, "I have something to discuss with you, Naama, daughter of Tsur. When you have finished your work, come to my house in the evening."

66

Naama answered, "I will do as you say."

Zidkiyohu turned and went off on his way, and Naama worked in the vineyard until dark.

After she had eaten and drunk, Naama rose and washed her face and put on her favorite dress and went to the house of Zidkiyohu. There she saw several important Elders, and her brother Merori standing before them with downcast face. He was very thin. His once upright and powerful figure was bent and shrunk. Filled with great compassion, Naama approached and greeted him. He opened his mouth to answer her, but he could not speak. He stood there, bowed low, without a word.

Then Zidkiyohu rose and said, "Naama, daughter of Tsur, your brother Merori has sinned grievously against you, but this day he came before the Elders and confessed his sin: that in deceit he took from you your father's inheritance. Now he repents his wickedness, for God has punished him greatly. Forgive him his sin and he will be pardoned."

Zidkiyohu then related to Naama and to the Elders who were present everything that had happened to Merori from the time that a certain old man had knocked on his door to ask for a night's lodging, and Merori had not let him in. Since then every night at midnight his money left his securely locked treasure chest, rose by itself, flew in the air in front of his eyes, and disappeared. When he reported this to his household, they did not believe him, even when he showed them what was missing in his treasure chest. They said an evil spirit was confusing him. He himself began to believe what they said and sought doctors, fortune tellers, and even asked the help of the dead through mediums. None could help him. After Naama had bought the piece of land near her house, he had had peace. But when the days of reaping and vintage had come, the evil spirit had returned.

During the harvest it was Merori's custom to sleep in the field with the reapers. And behold! During the first night at midnight he saw five sheaves, the best and the fullest in his field, rise, stand, and fly! They flew before his eyes and were gone! The same thing happened the second night and the third. He called to his boys, who were asleep in the field not far from him, and showed them the flying sheaves. They looked at him with bewildered faces—they saw nothing.

And one night, when the sheaves began to fly in the air, he got up and followed them and saw that they came to the piece of land belonging to Naama. They descended into the field and arranged themselves in a row near her own sheaves, as though an invisible hand were placing them there. He followed them the next night, and all the succeeding nights until the end of the harvest. Each night he saw the same thing.

It was the same with the vintage. Bunches of grapes and olives were carried off before his eyes and flew in the air like birds. He followed them until they reached the branches of the vines and olive trees of his sister. Then his heart knew, then he understood, that it was the hand of God at work. Because he had deceitfully taken his father's inheritance from his sister, Naama, God was taking his inheritance from him.

"All these things I relate to you, word for word from the mouth of Merori. He now stands before you. But what I do not understand is this: Naama, daughter of Tsur, saw that her sheaves, her olives and grapes were being doubled, and yet she did not come to us, the Elders. She said nothing to us. So, Naama, I summoned you. Now stand up and tell us the truth, so that we may know and understand all this, and know what words to use in righteousness and justice."

Then Naama rose and told Zidkiyohu and the Elders everything from beginning to end. She told about the old man, about the coin, and about

Merori embraced his sister . . .

the field. But she did not know from whom the money came, or the sheaves and clusters of olives and grapes. Moreover, she had been amazed that the sheaves had come to her, since she had not asked the coin for anything since the day she had bought the field.

The Elders listened to her words and said, "God is perfect in His work, and all His deeds are truth and righteousness."

After that Merori embraced his sister, kissed her, and wept, and she also wept. He gave her her share of her father's inheritance, according to law, and they made peace between them.

When the villagers heard all about this, they were very happy, praised the Lord for His goodness, and said, "Now we have perfect peace here. The peace and truth to which we were always accustomed will ever be in our midst, for there is no longer any evil in our dwellings."

This affair was recorded in a book and sealed with the seal of Zidkiyohu, the village Elder, so that future generations might know of it and act in kindness and justice toward the stranger and the wanderer.